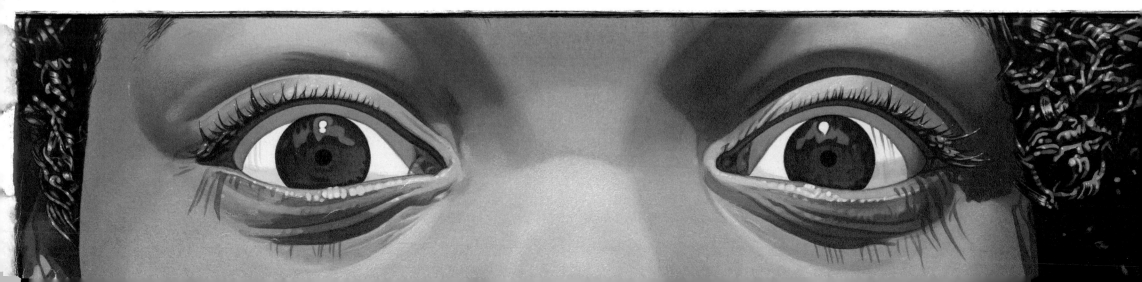

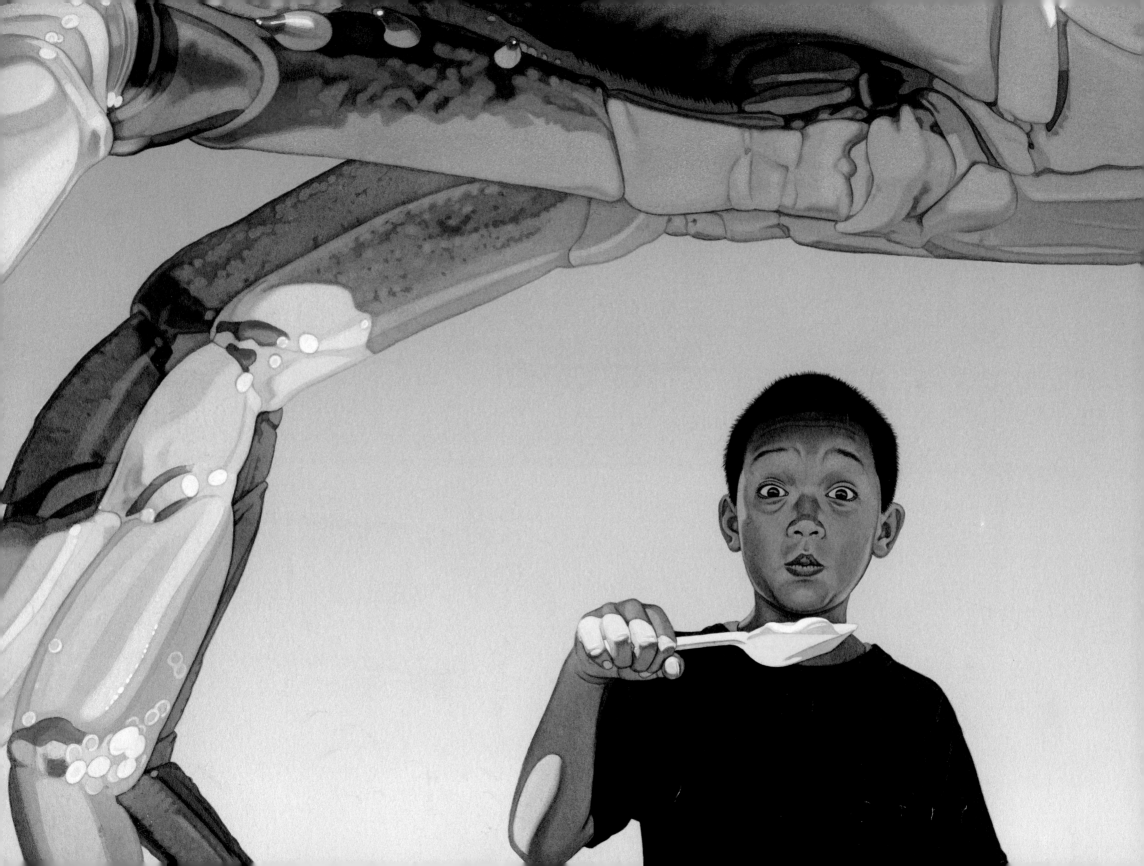

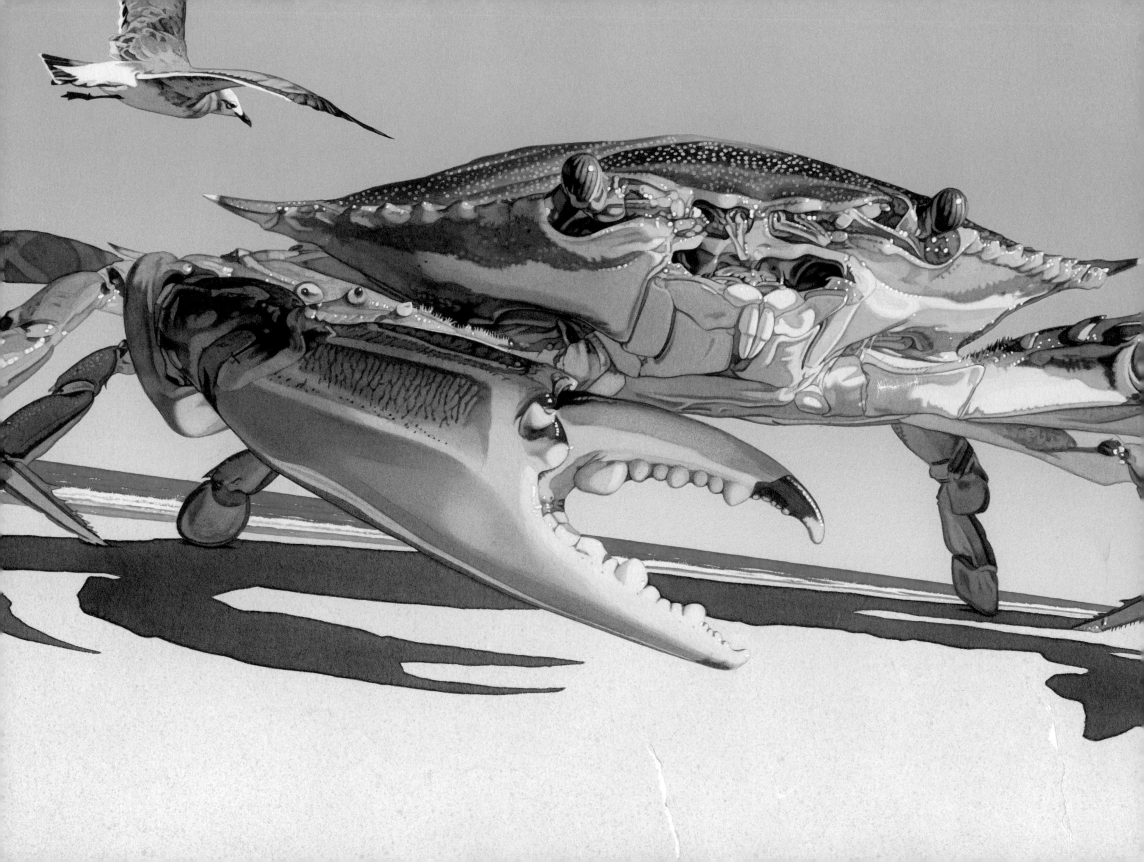

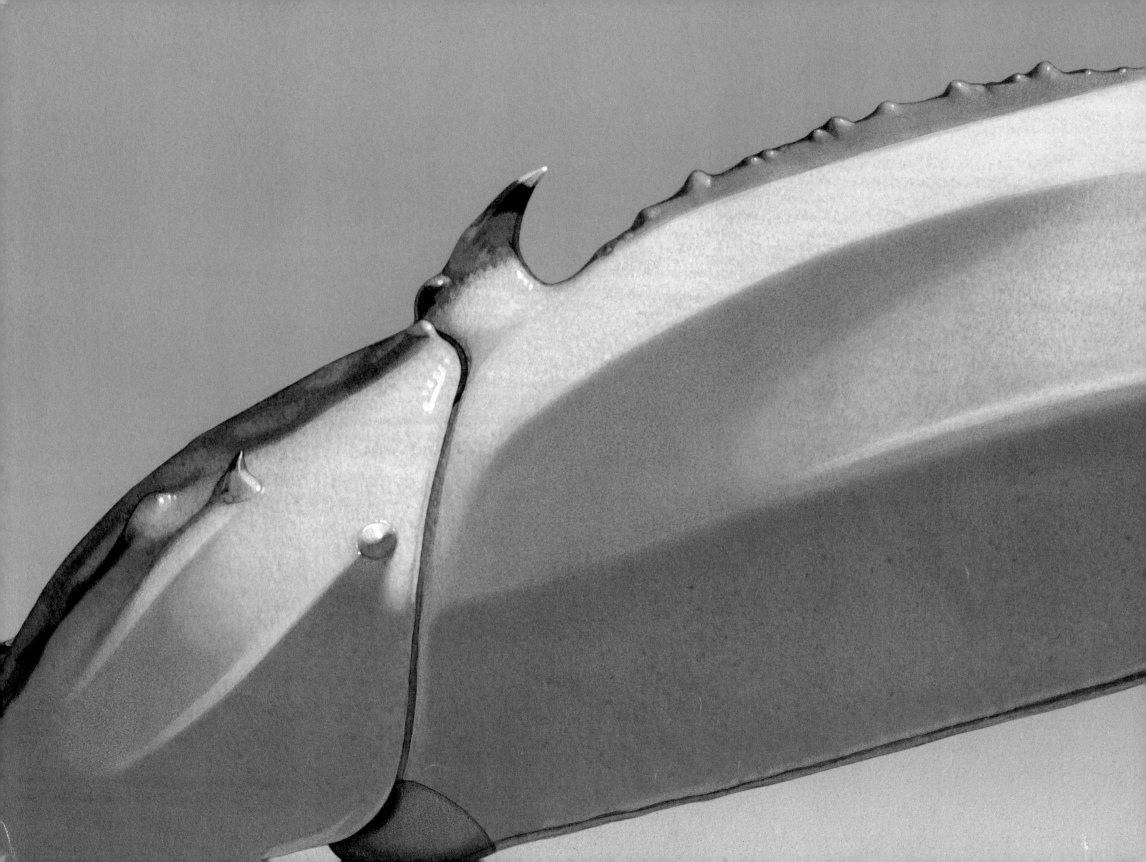

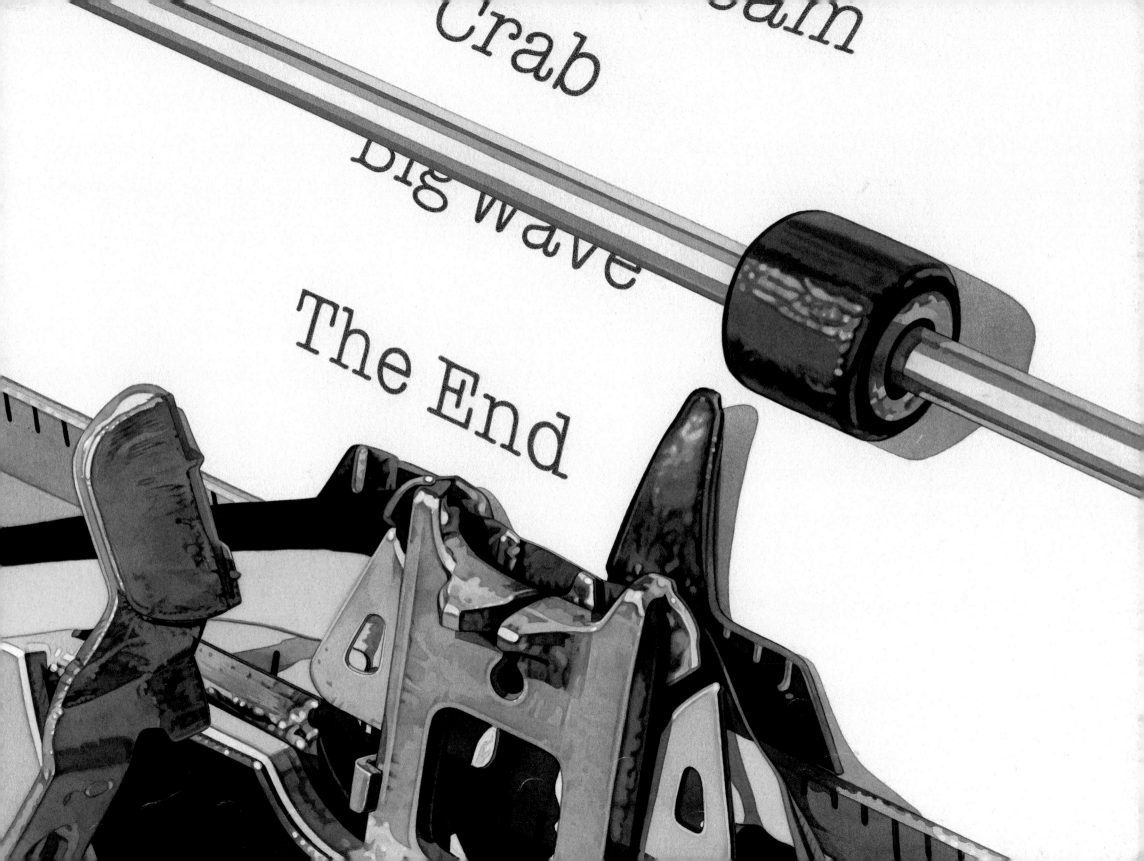

This book is dedicated with love to Diann and the power of the WORD.
Special thanks to Margery Cuyler for believing in imagination.

Published by Two Lions, New York | www.apub.com

Amazon, the Amazon logo, and Two Lions are trademarks of
Amazon.com, Inc., or its affiliates.

ISBN-13: 9781477849750 (hardcover)
ISBN-10: 1477849750 (hardcover)

ISBN-13: 9781503954991 (paperback)
ISBN-10: 1503954994 (paperback)

Bill Thomson created a handmade model of a bumblebee
before beginning his artwork. Using traditional painting
techniques, he meticulously painted each illustration by hand
with acrylic paint and colored pencils. His illustrations are
not photographs or computer-generated images.

Book design by Abby Dening
Printed in China
First edition

10 9 8 7 6 5 4 3 2 1

two lions

SPELLING BEE